# THE HUGHES DISPATCH

Copyright © 2023 Hughes Academy All rights reserved

The characters and events portrayed in this book are fictitious. Any similarity to real persons, living or dead, is coincidental and not intended by the authors.

No part of this book may be reproduced, or stored in a retrieval system, or transmitted in any form or by any means, electronic, mechanical, photocopying, recording, or otherwise, without express written permission of the publisher.

ISBN-13: 9798386258092

Cover design by: Sophie Gwaltney and Madeline Barker
Printed in the United States of America

# Contents

*Jordan Finlay* **9** Foreward
*Patrick Burell* **11** Introduction
*& Toni Heyward*

## The Book of Light

*Alana Cortes* **15** Blossoming Spring
*Alondra Rodriguez Rosales* **17** The Moon and The Sun
*EJ Ortiz Torres* **18** Ode to a Cat Named Whiskers
*Max Dotson* **21** The World Beyond
*Ana Humes* **22** Stars
*Matthew Maldonado* **24** Thunder in the Sky
*Sabriya Jenkins* **27** Spring
*Kelly Pablo* **28** Winter
*Harper Jacobs* **30** A Turn for the Worst
*Sadie Vukoder-Ash* **31** Window
*Siena Ridolfo* **33** The Colder Times
*Jessie Hicks* **35** Counting down the days
*Alana Cortes* **37** beautiful outside
*Sarah Moniot* **39** Uprooted Promises

## The Book of Darkness

*Omega Brewster* **50** 3-Legged Dead
*Emery Jorgensen* **52** Where The Whispers Roam
*Eva Menendez* **55** Cold is Black
*Audrey Shockley* **56** Soloing Life
*Alondra Rodriguez Rosales* **61** Ignored, But Not By Choice
*Siena Ridolfo* **65** Beneath the Surface
*Audrey Shockley* **69** The Woman I Married

# The Book of Truths

| | | |
|---|---|---|
| *Edward Bastida Villa & Diego Rangel* | 77 | Stories Heard from Latinos |
| *Ryan Hayes* | 79 | Alluring Almond Amber Eyes |
| *Alana Cortes* | 81 | To my friends |
| *Josh Nielsen* | 83 | Why I Dislike My Job |
| *Sadie Vukoder-Ash* | 85 | One Day |
| *Ansley Peace* | 86 | Nuclear Life |
| *Alejandra Zepeda-Zelaya* | 87 | Jealousy |
| *Siri Vanmall* | 88 | Happy Diwali |
| *Emery Jorgensen* | 89 | Hang in there! |
| *Alejandra Zepeda-Zelaya* | 91 | Home |
| *Tarahji Anderson* | 92 | We are all equal |
| *Andrew Harson* | 94 | Deep |
| *Dominick Prietti* | 96 | I Dream |
| *Alex Smith* | 97 | A Shade of Power |
| *Jorja Holmes* | 99 | The Locket |
| *Anouk Bridges* | 103 | Invaded |
| *Alejandra Zepeda-Zelaya* | 108 | Getting older |
| *Haven Dendy* | 109 | Life is a Beauty |
| *Treasure Williams* | 110 | A Peaceful Slumber |
| *Anouk Bridges* | 112 | Mama's Perfumes |
| *Honesti McKinney-Sullivan* | 113 | Friend, Friend |
| *Anouk Bridges* | 115 | The Four |
| *Ryan Hayes* | 125 | To the One I Lost |
| *Patrick Burell & Toni Heyward* | 135 | Acknowledgements |

# List of Illustrations

## Cover
Sophie Gwaltney    Hughes in Springtime
& Madeline Barker

## Chapter Titles
Helen Wolfe   13   The Book of Light
Harper Jacobs   47   The Book of Darkness
Susannah Dunbar   75   The Book of Truths

## Illustrations
Sally Roe   16   The Moon and The Sun
Mikayla Moore   19   Ode to a Cat Named Whiskers
Eliot Cizon   20   The World Beyond
Ana Humes   23   Stars
Genesis Thomas   25   Thunder in the Sky
Emery Jorgensen   26   Spring
Olivia Cannon   29   Winter
Lucy Mac Brown   32   The Colder Times
LillyAnn Talley   34   Counting down the days
Sarah Moniot   38   Uprooted Promises
Bitia Apolonio Villanueva   49   In the Dark
Bitia Apolonio Villanueva   51   3-Legged Dead
Emery Jorgensen   53   Where The Whispers Roam
Sarah Moniot   54   Cold is Black
Alondra Rodriguez Rosales   62   Ignored, but not by choice
Peyton Case   67   Beneath the Surface
Ryan Hayes   78   Alluring Almond Amber Eyes
Jazmin Smith   82   Why I Dislike My Job
Camillia San   84   One Day
Alysia Magarino   90   Home
Natalie Dixon   93   We are all equal
Jayla Johnson   95   Deep
Jay Mitchell   98   The Locket
Anouk Bridges   102   Invaded
Xian Minne   111   A Peaceful Slumber
Anouk Bridges   114   The Four
Ryan Hayes   124   To the One I Lost

"The artist is the confidant of nature, flowers carry on dialogues with him through the graceful bending of their stems and the harmoniously tinted nuances of their blossoms. Every flower has a cordial word which nature directs towards him."

– **Auguste Rodin**

# Foreward

The middle school experience is all about exploring interests, discovering passions, and developing the mindset that is needed for success in high school and beyond. At Hughes Academy, we believe that providing students with unique opportunities to explore their interests beyond the traditional classroom setting is critical to their personal and academic development. As the Principal at Hughes Academy, it is my honor and privilege to support The Hughes Dispatch.

This project was developed by one of our talented educators, Mr. Burell, who has shown incredible ambition and creativity in the creation of this incredible collection of student work. He and his colleagues, most notably Mrs. Heyward with whom he co-teaches in a 7th-grade English and Language Arts class, inspired students to submit their original works in this first ever publication from Hughes Academy. These students poured their heart and soul into this series of short stories and poems which are sure to move any reader. Mr. Burell and Mrs. Heyward screened over one hundred submissions to curate this incredible collection of original student works. After spending the last sixteen years serving thousands of students and hundreds of teachers in middle schools throughout Greenville County, I can say with confidence that I have never come across such an impressive example of writing talent. I believe you'll find our first edition of The Hughes Dispatch to be thought provoking, funny, and insightful.

When students are given the opportunity to write freely about topics that interest them, we see their creativity and passion shine through in their work. As you read this carefully selected group of writing samples from our students, it may be hard to believe that eleven to fourteen year olds have produced such quality writing.

However, this is more than just a collection of short stories and poems from middle school students. The Hughes Dispatch represents a collaborative effort engaging an entire community through writing and art. The illustrations which complement the writing throughout this collection are also original works of art created by Hughes Academy students and inspired by the writings of their classmates. As Principal of the school, it fills me with pride to see the talents and interests of our diverse student body combine to enhance one another and provide our school community with authentic examples of what can be accomplished when we collaborate to accomplish a common goal.

As legendary coach and educator, John Wooden once said, "Success is the peace of mind which can only be attained through the self-satisfaction of knowing you've done the best of which you are capable." The artists and authors featured in The Hughes Dispatch exemplified this approach in their work. It's not about how many copies are sold, or how much attention they might gain, but instead, it was simply about expressing themselves in unique ways and being fully engaged in the process. They understood that the journey itself is the destination. Join us as we embark through this beautiful display of student creativity.

Jordan Finlay  
*March 2023*

# Introduction

Welcome to the inaugural edition of The Hughes Dispatch!

This book is both a response to and an outpouring of the creativity that is present here at Hughes Academy. As we pored over the pages of our students' work last fall, we realized that the complexity and thoughtfulness of our students' writing needed more than just an outlet: it needed somewhere to be put on display. Out of this need was birthed the book you now hold.

The book is divided into three sections— The Book of Light, The Book of Darkness, and The Book of Truths. Each book takes readers on a journey through many emotions and the depth of our students' imaginations.

### *The Book of Light*
Just as the sun illuminates our world and all that it encompasses, The Book of Light is a beacon showcasing the beauty that is Mother Nature, while also capturing the moments of life that make up the fondest of memories. A refreshing assortment of seasonal pieces and blissful moments in time, colored by an ambiance of vivid depictions help paint a radiant landscape of the human experience. Whether it's a blossoming flower, a furry companion or a moment of reflection, the works here captivate happiness and cultivate optimism. The poems and short stories in this book capture the essence of light and life. The works illustrate that our universe is a canvas upon which stories begin to take shape, sculpting the world around us.

### *The Book of Darkness*
The Book of Darkness examines the voids that exist in the absence of light and probes the obscurities that are present within the world. As you plummet into this black hole, prepare for a cold chill of tales that unveil sorrow and uncover pain, highlighting the somber experiences of existence. The chronicles featured here acknowledge the reality of broken spirits, tainted memories and the finality of existence. Like a withering petal, breaths that slowly drift away become a focal point.

### *The Book of Truths*
Lastly, in The Book of Truths, readers will explore the many facets of human experience. In this collection, you will journey over great lands, witness epic battles, and wrestle with the deep struggles of everyday life. These poems and stories invite you to wrestle with what it means to belong, to question how you see the world, to face your insecurities, and to seek the true meaning of friendship. Whether real or imagined, these stories will inspire you and leave you with a deeper appreciation for the complexity of the human condition.

Art is in many ways a communal endeavor. No one walks alone through this life. The works you'll find in these pages are a testament to the support and encouragement provided by our entire community, including teachers, administrators, staff, parents, grandparents, uncles, brothers, sisters, local leaders, and the wonderful people that surrounds this school. We created this book not only to showcase our students' talent, but also to celebrate the community that made it possible.

Patrick Burell
Toni Heyward
*March 2023*

**Blossoming Spring**
By Alana Cortes

Wind has awoken
The trees and sprouts, old and young
Life begins anew

Buds yearn to blossom
Delicate petals unfurl
Beauty is unveiled

As the flowers bloom
Breeze gently flows through the sky
Guiding lonely clouds

Drifting through meadows
No shadow in the sunlight
Smiling at the leaves

Realization
Nature softly whispering
Saying "spring is here"

**The Moon and The Sun**
By Alondra Rodriguez Rosales

The moon shines bright during the night,
While the sun shines through the day.
Opposites intertwined by fate,
Their love is so great, yet forbidden.
The sun will burn everything if it is too happy,
It will freeze everything if it is heartbroken.
The moon can never give the sun a true answer,
For if she did things would end in disaster.

**Ode to a Cat Named Whiskers**
By Ej Ortiz Torres

His soft orange tabby fur
Reminds me of fluffy blankets

His beautiful yellow eyes
Reminds of the sun

When it's time to feed him
He waits patiently

He likes to go behind the blinds
and look out the window

And purrs when he's sleeping
His purr is like a song

Breath purr
Breath purr

He likes to sleep on anything
He's calm and plays during the daytime

At night he's a maniac
And has an advantage
with night vision
to get our legs

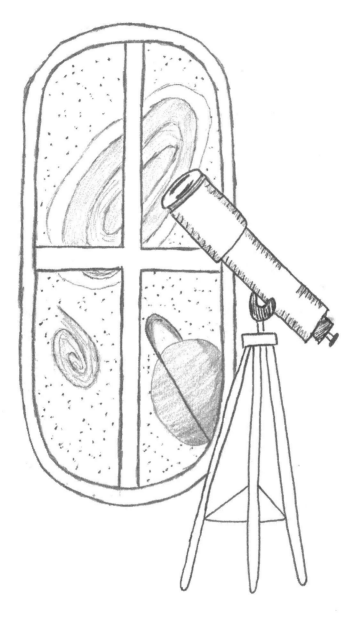

**The World Beyond**
By Max Dotson

Sometimes the mind wonders,

What is in the world beyond?
The massive expanse above and around the Earth.

Full of stars and planets,
Shining like holes in the sky.

The answer lies above,
If closely examined.

Galaxies, larger than imaginable,
Solar systems, full of planets and asteroids,
The absolute beauty of space and the world beyond.

Like a deer leaping through a field,
The stars leap through our sky every night, unnoticed.

Like a work of art full of colors,
There's nebulae of plum,
And stars of tangerine.

Then there's us,
A pale blue dot in the world beyond.

**Stars**
By Ana Humes

Always like a light
Glistening as diamonds
Always in the night
Savoring the silence
Always near
But never always seen
Stars are like fairies
The angels of dreams.
Look up at those diamonds
As the forest of stars gleam,
Because after all
they could give you what you need.

**Thunder in the Sky**
By Matthew Maldonado

The storm yelled across the whole city.
Mother Nature felt terrible grief
For the earth that was once pretty.

The fighting, the war,
What can we do?
The sky is now brown, '
Not the pretty silk blue.

Mother gets worried sick about it,
There's not much time.
She just wishes the people
Had a change of mind.

The oceans filled to the top with trash,
The once blue sky filled with gas.

Mother nature was clearly upset,
You could see it too.
The clouds form a frown,
Almost just like you.

"Please stop!" Mother Nature cries.
But unfortunately, to us
It just sounded like thunder in the sky.

**Spring**
By Sabriya Jenkins

Sleeping inside of the house all night.
Partying with friends.
Riding bikes with family.
In a field of flowers.
Not feeling well.
Going on vacation.

**Winter**
By Kelly Pablo

Warm clothes
Cold frost ices
Hot cocoa and marshmallows
Snow ices
Snow flakes
Snow angels
Playing in the snow
Having fun

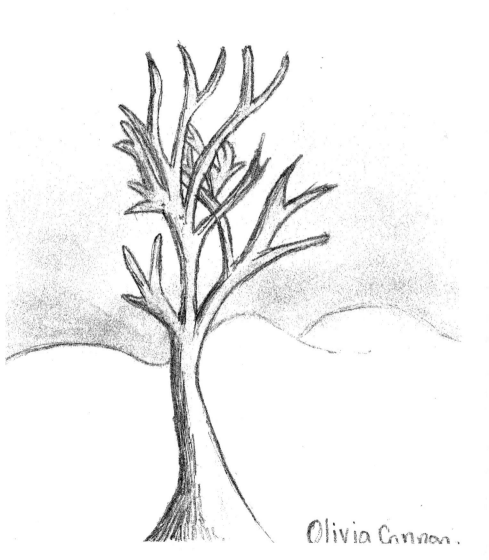

**A Turn for the Worst**
By Harper Jacobs

Climate change is a calamity.
You need to be careful around it, or it will get worse.
To help this catastrophe, you can do many things

You can ride a bike or walk places,
Or recycle your trash.
You can turn the lights off when you are not using them,
Or take shorter showers.

This will end our world if we are not careful
I am sure you don't want that to happen.
Creatures will vanish like magic,
Places will go away.

The world will be dull and depressing.
It will end up like a pile of trash.
And that would be sad


So change things

so that future generations

won't have to experience

this pain.

Please!

**Window**
By Sadie Vukoder-Ash

Always looking at life
through a window
is never enough.
Buried deep down
into the internet
is stalling time.
Much rather be outside
drinking a drink
that was saturated with lime.
Such a beautiful day
the sun is shining,
birds thrive,
oh what a time to be
Alive.

But instead,
you're looking at life through a window.

Instead of playing with neighborhood kids,
or running around, not a care in the world.
But instead, watching time go by looking at your phone.

Wouldn't you much rather be outside?
80° weather, nice
cold drink in your hand,
soaking up the sun.

But you're too busy
on your phone to even acknowledge
the world around you,
Let alone your own tone.

**The Colder Times**
By Siena Ridolfo

Red and orange leaves on the ground
White snow falling all around
I walk through depressed trees
While flowers begin to freeze

This place always looks so different,
In the cold times, when the flowers are no longer magnificent
It's covered in blank and icy snow
Where the pink trees used to show

Although the colors are gone
And the spry, green plants have withdrawn
The winter does have its wonder,
In the quiet while everything is in a slumber

The bustling action of the world
Calms down as winter unfolds.
The chaos of it all
Turns into a quiet, tranquil song.

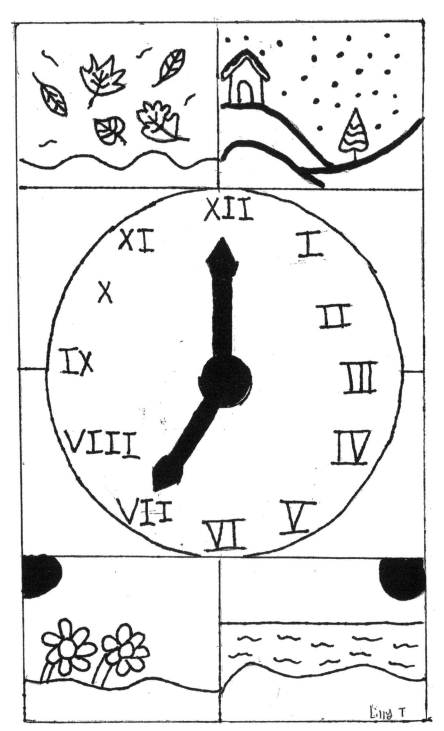

**Counting down the days**
By Jessie Hicks

In the summer,
Everyone looks forward to fall.

They look forward to when the leaves
turn red and orange,
when football season starts,
Halloween,
thanksgiving,
pumpkin pie,
and anything with cinnamon.

When fall comes,
Everyone looks forward to winter.

When every coffee shop
is playing Christmas music,
and candy canes are stuffed in mason jars.
When candles are lit on the menorah.
When your snow boots are sitting by their door (Just in case.)

When winter comes,
Everyone looks forward to spring.

When they walk through meadows of flowers
and watch the rain pelting on their window, a blurry mess,
that still looks cozy and comforting.

But when spring comes,
Everyone looks forward to summer.

When the pools open up,
boats sip down the lake,
and people wheel their beach carts out to the sand,
feeling the sensation of the warm beachy air.

Now I'm dancing through a flower meadow,
and later I'll watch the rain on my window.
I'm pondering many different things,
but only about what I've been doing this spring

**beautiful outside**
By Alana Cortes

Staring out the window
Into the soft but bright
Ocean of the sky

Clouded with the fluffy blossoms
Gracefully decorating
Delicate branches

The sun's loving gaze
Emerges for a moment
Illuminating the beauty

Gently swaying
Waving to their lovers
Lost in dreamy admiration

Unbothered by mortal worries
Calmly sprouting in their own time
Unconsciously beckoning

Defying reality
Somehow carelessly but sweetly
Reaching for eternity
In a precious moment

**Uprooted Promises**
By Sarah Moniot

Long ago, when the world was still young and flourishing, a great drought fell upon the lands. None were more poorly affected than the tall and mighty beings of Oakwood Forest. When before, their elegant limbs reached for the stars, leaves soaked in moonlight, now the whole wood stank of rot and decay.

And as if the dry soil and parched sky had caught and spread like wildfire, all manor of creatures fled the Oakwood's withering grasp.

Of course, not all of them could afford the tiresome journey. A mother bird, her once plump body growing thinner with every passing season, was forced to stay behind. She knew her children's ever-persistent cries of hunger would be quieted if they left the familiar comfort of the now shriveled forest. As they huddled close in their half-rotted log, the majestic woods came crashing down around them.

Just a few short weeks after their fall, all evidence of the woods' once great presence had disappeared. The flies and mushrooms, having been starved of death for all those years, did not let the carcasses of Oakwood go to waste.

The mother bird and her chicks, who could live on nuts and seeds for only so long, eventually ventured out into the woods to begin the search for food. Although they could no longer hear the scampering of mice or the almost silent trail of earthworms, they happened upon a bit of life in the browning underbrush. Mother Bird gave a little chirp of astonishment when she saw what looked like a miniature oakwood sapling struggling to gain purchase among the death surrounding it, for she could scarcely remember the last taste of fresh leaves on her tongue.

"It's a pity no one else will glimpse this morsel of color before it's gone," murmured Mother Bird as she hopped over to snatch a leaf from its bough. Oh, how she'd missed those great oaks and their almost too sweet buds. She could already feel the curious fragrance cloying her- "Were you attempting to eat me?!" shouted the sapling, leaves bristling.

Much to his mother's growing disbelief, the youngest of the three chicks offered up a quick reply, "You'll have to forgive my mother. We've all been terribly hungry of late, and she'd probably eat anything that isn't the color of rotting acorns," He leaned in closer, as if to tell a naughty secret, "Just between you and me, I think she tried to eat my brother Roj once- to be fair, he looked quite a bit like a strawberry at the time but-" He was abruptly cut off by a stern peck of warning atop his head. "Come, children," Mother Bird retorted severely, herding them away. The eldest of the two followed obediently, but the latter, most childlike of the trio lingered, not yet fully grasping the extent of his mother's temperament.

"Wait!" cried the plant in the clipped tone of forest folk. It was hard to say of course, looking back, but surely the lanky thing wouldn't have called out to the lot of them if not for the youngest's mournful glance behind him.

"I- I really didn't mean to sound callous, it's just that no one ever comes to this part of the thicket, and- well there's not really anyone to talk to but my own dead leaves." Mother Bird, about to start on her way, paused when she heard the sapling call out a second time, "Please! Don't go! I'll make you a deal: you can eat one of my leaves each week, if only you'll just stay a while, and bring me a bit of water from time to time- my leaves are awfully parched, what with the recent lack of rains."

"If I agree," replied Mother Bird cautiously, and the sprout instantly perked up at her words. "If I agree, how do I know you won't just shake us off your branches in the night?"

The sprout hesitated for a long moment before answering, "I don't know how or why, but no lie I try to utter can pass from my body."

With a second glance back at her offspring, Mother Bird agreed, for even those that are bitter can be moved by the simple kindness of others. Needless to say, her motives didn't just surface from the goodness of her heart. She still desperately wanted a taste of those candied leaves.

"Do you have a name, sapling, or would you prefer us to call you our weekday meal?" Mother Bird inquired, a hint of mockery marring her tone.

"No one cared to name me, for I was alone from the moment my roots reached into the dirt." said the plant, its branches drooping ever so slightly.

"No matter," remarked Mother Bird flippantly, "I will call you Tree after the treacle sweet sap that must run through your veins."

Mother Bird, never one to dance around a troublesome subject, looked the newly dubbed plant up and down before pointedly asking, "Well? It's been a week, shouldn't I be allowed to eat you by now?"

Tree, sensing the foul mood wafting off her in angry, pulsing waves, silently lowered one of his branches without argument.

Without hesitation, Mother Bird expertly plucked off an especially bright leaf in one fell swoop. Try as he might, Tree couldn't help letting out a cry of pain. All things considered, it was a somewhat considerable show of restraint, for having a limb torn from one's body is no small matter.

Knowing the youngest chick- who they had taken to calling Alister- would have quite a mouthful to say about the matter, Mother Bird cast her eyes down, almost as if she could hear the disapproving chirps of his voice. Trying to hide his pained expression, Tree grimaced a little as Mother Bird padded over to the now leafless branch, dripping shining, amber sap and wrapped an old bit of spider web around the break.

"Can't have you dying on me before I'm paid in full." She had intended her tone to be harsh, but that didn't stop the kindness from seeping through.

That season, the rains came without warning.

Rose, being the oldest and thinking herself the most intelligent, was the first to point out the light drizzle that had begun to accompany them each morning. Roj didn't seem to care much- like Tree, the dry climate irked him to no end. Naturally, Alister could not stop complaining about his wet feathers after Rose first mentioned the damp weather.

Nevertheless, their flying lessons went on as planned. They had taken to leaping off one of Tree's lower branches- which were starting to become too far and in between, for the rains caused him to shoot into the gloomy sky at an alarming pace, growing taller by the hour. They could have flown off of the many other saplings Tree had produced over the past few weeks of course, but he had insisted, saying his limbs were finer than all the rest.

"Mother," whined Alister, dragging out the syllables, "Why must we fly in the rain? I'm damp enough as it is."

"Be grateful for your wings, child, as only us birds can soar in the sky," reprimanded Mother Bird primly, puffing her rumpled feathers slightly.

But before she could scold him any longer, Tree spoke loudly, his branches quivering with excitement, "I must be a bird then! I soar in the sky just as much as any of you!"

"Don't be silly, Tree," Mother Bird chided, "You don't fly! You are but a plant, and nothing should possess you to be anything but that- to stand there and provide a home for the rest of us is to be who you are."

It was Roj who finally spoke, "I do not believe what we are born as should be what defines us." As if the rains had felt the significance of the moment, it began to fall in larger, more frequent drops, insistent upon ruining the momentous occasion.

The soggy birds were eventually forced to find shelter in the nest sequestered in Tree's branches; it had become quite dense after Mother Bird had neglected to mention their weekly deal. The silver pool of water around his trunk was rising much too briskly for his taste. The large onslaught of various forest animals splashing in the muck towards him seemed to have the same mindset prior to skidding to a halt below him.

"Great Tree!" clamored a large deer, "Please let us find cover from the floods in your exceptional branches! We will make sure your roots are never thirsty, that you are never harmed, if only you'll protect us from the floods!"

"I will allow you to rest in my branches and that of my kin

when there are any waters that may trouble you, but you must remember to uphold your promise," boomed Tree, attempting to sound as foreboding as possible. The animals nodded solemnly, signaling Tree to lower his many limbs. They gracefully leaped into his outstretched arms, the more sizable creatures tottering precariously before finally settling.

The rains did not cease for three days, the floods remaining double that before finally receding. The forest's newest residents thanked Tree for his help, staying close so as to offer water when the dry season came back around.

The seasons passed more or less uneventfully, animals slowly trickling back into the forest, like sand to an hourglass. They always bargained for the Tree's protection, offering treasures of all sorts, though the Tree found no reason to deny anyone entrance. It was more of a formality now than anything else. He recognised most all of the newcomers, except a strange being who approached him with the skin of a grizzly bear draped across his broad shoulders.

"Great Tree!" he called, "Please let us find shelter in a quiet corner of your exceptional forest! We will make sure your soil is always fertile, that you are never harmed, if only you'll grant us entrance!"

"I will allow you to remain in my forest, but you must remember to uphold your promise," rumbled Tree, his voice more ominous than the first time he'd spoken words not too different from those just said. Primarily because of curiosity, Tree asked, "What are you?"

"I am a man, Great Tree, one of many." the man answered with the respect Tree had become accustomed to. He retrieved a bottle from some hidden place on his person before continuing, "I have created a concoction to aid the growth of your roots. If you'd like, I could pour it at the base of your trunk."

Tree rustled his branches in approval- careful not to disturb the many birds resting on them- and with that, the man stepped forward to pour his fertilizer. He did not think to thank the man, because he could scarcely speak when his roots absorbed the syrupy sweetness. It was like feeling everything and nothing all at once. The sounds of chirping birds quieted to a soft caress, he hadn't much cared for their pointless chatter after Mother Bird and her chicks had slowly trickled away, but the birds were always drawn to his branches like moths to a flame. Before he knew it, the sensation dulled, cloudless sky, already the color of a raven's wing.

The man came again the next morning to pour his tincture into the soil, and once more, Tree tasted that wonderful syrupy sweetness, time slipping away again.

He came thrice more times before Tree began to notice his bearer branches, the silence that seemed to douse everything like a wet blanket. Where were all the birds? Why weren't the crickets chirping? Had the forest shrunk or was his vision going awry? What had happened to the trees that had before risen up all around him? He tried to call out, but a familiar sweetness dampened his voice.

A group of men, looking as if the sun had ceased shining on their gray faces, drew nearer, the tallest of them brandishing a silver ax. Tree tried to call out to them, but his branches were stiff, leaves only moving a fraction of an inch.

The Great Tree, now the first and last of his kind, who had survived drought, flood and all manner of terrible things, was cut down by a lone blade swung by the first of many liars.

## Reader Beware

The stories that lie ahead may chill you to the bone, dear reader. Within these pages, you will find tales of death, murder, and other disturbing themes that may not be suitable for the faint of heart. If you are easily disturbed or unsettled by such content, we advise you to skip this section. Consider yourself warned.

## 3-Legged Dead
By Omega Brewster

It was a dark and stormy night.

There was a dog that had 3 legs

And there was another dog with no legs.

There was a creepy dog house

At the end of the street.

The dog with three legs said, "we should go check it out."

The dog with no legs said, "maybe we shouldn't."

But they went anyway.

When they got to the house the dog with 3 legs said,

"let's go up stairs."

The dog with no legs said, "I can't."

So the dog with 3 legs went up there by himself.

And when he got on the final step he fell backwards

and died.

And at the end when he fell down

The dog with no legs was standing on top of the stairs

laughing.

He had been a ghost the entire time.

**Where The Whispers Roam**
By Emery Jorgensen

There will come many a time in your life
When whispers show and urge you to follow
And in that time of deep and vengeful strife
You may chase your desire so hollow
Cloudy skies turn into a brutal storm
And bright fields to forests of starless night
Wind wails around you, dark thoughts start to swarm
But it still assures you are in the right
Down the winding path, trees begin to shake
Things begin to warp like a ripple in a pond
And then it swallows you up like a snake
Chasing those whispers, now you're too far gone
Clouds could have cleared, but in their worldwide home
Seems you've lost yourself where the whispers roam

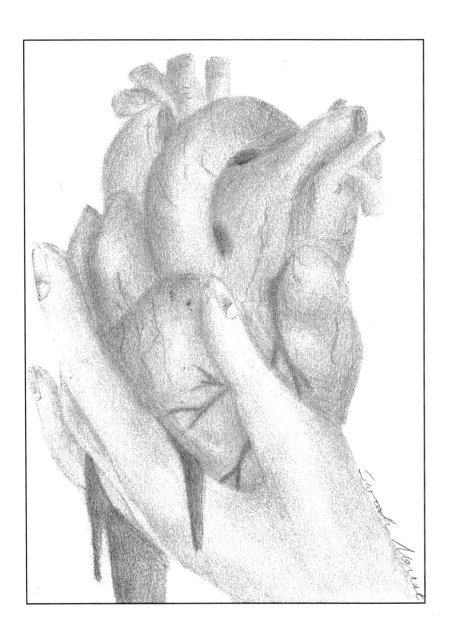

**Cold is Black**
By Eva Menendez

Gripping cold
Gnawing hunger
Grasping at my belly
Will I ever be full?
Mother, father, ban from shadowclan heart

Left to die out here all alone
Tom and she-cat to care after me
Will it be enough?
Cold is growing
Fear is piling

My eyes only see black
Will I ever see light?
Mother's warmth is growing farther
Breath is falling
I can't see father
What will be left?

Life is slipping away
I breathe one last breath
Whispering fills my head
With all that is left I say
"I hope you have a nice life"
Then the world goes black

**Soloing Life**
By Audrey Shockley

TV reporters all around the region came to film the free solo of Robert Clinton. It was a cold day in January 2046. Robert Clinton was a tall man with a lanky build, yet toned and muscular arms. He had long blonde hair, gray eyes, and a stubble beard growing on his chin. He had a very stern concentrated face and a chiseled jawline. He was dressed in jeans and a long T-shirt.

TV reporters gathered around Robert while he tried to prepare. Eyes all around the world were on him. He was about to free solo El Capitan; only 1 man has done it before, 44 others have attempted, but it didn't go so well.

David Clinton, Robert's brother, ushered the reporters away to give him some space. "How are you feeling?" David asked.

Robert continued to focus on his pushups, "I'm ready. I just need a moment to breathe." Robert jumped up, "David, you're my older brother, so let me be honest. I am scared, really scared. I'm afraid I'm going to die but I also don't really mind if I do."

A look of concern flashed in David's eyes, "What do you mean?"

David could tell Robert was thinking of his late wife Julia. Julia was a beautiful, elegant woman. She had long brown wavy hair and brown eyes. Those eyes had lit up Robert's life the first time he saw them.

Robert met Julia in college when she came to the wrong class. Julia was lost and Robert offered to give her a tour of the school. Afterward, Robert drove both of them to town for some dinner. Ever since then, he'd been head over heels for her.

Robert would always obsess over her smile. It lifted her cheekbones and she had the most perfect teeth; so white you could see your reflection in them. In Robert's eyes, her dimples were the cutest sight on the planet.

They had a wedding where they got married and even were going to have a kid, but 5 months into the pregnancy Julia got into a car accident. She passed from her injuries and so did the baby. Robert was devastated. His whole life has been taken away. His world shattered and he lost all hope for a better life.

Robert used to be a successful businessman, but when Julia died he quit his job. Wanting to do something to add thrill to his life, he grew his hair long and started free soloing.

"I'm ready to die," Robert told his brother. "I mean, I'm not trying to die, I'm just not scared if it happens. Sure it would be nice if I lived and made history, but if I don't, oh well."

David stood there silently, not able to mutter a word. He looked at Robert's stern face, that face had never changed since his wife's funeral. Emotionless, cold eyes. His face had been so lively once, it brought joy to everyone nearby. Now it was just a stare, a piercing stare.

"Well," David said, finally mustering up the words he wanted to say. "Please be careful. I want you to be safe, I need you."

Robert nodded. "I have to go now," he said and started to walk away.

"Wait! Robby!" David yelled. Robby turned around to face

him. "I love you kid," David said.
A spark of emotion ran through Robert's eyes, but it quickly went away with a blink. Robert nodded at his brother in response and tried to suppress his smile. Those words brought joy to Robert.

He wanted to beat the record. He wanted to solo El Capitan in 3 hours. A news reporter came up to him, "What makes you think you can beat Alex Honnold's time of 3 hours and 56 minutes with no practice and little experience? Alex had to practice for 6 weeks with rope to understand the perimeter. What makes you think you can do this? Why are you doing this?"

"I admire Alex. He is an inspiration to me. I have nothing but respect for him, so this is not out of resentment or bad blood, but Alex had his girlfriend. He had somebody who depended on him so he had to take his time and be careful. He took the greatest risk in history but he still had something to live for. I don't." Robert replied with no hesitation. He'd prepared for that question.

The crowd fell silent. "Well," the news reporter replied, choking on tears. "I'm sorry to hear that, I wish you the best of luck." The two men shook hands.

He started the climb, the crowd watching in awe as he boosted up the mountain at record speeds. His hands were numb from the cold but he kept going. He kept going fast and took every risk in the book, all the right moves.

About half an hour into the climb, he felt something in one of the crevices. Robert stopped and fiddled with it under his fingers. He pulled it out and it was a green gem. It reflected lots of light into his eyes. Attached was a note.

The note said to make any wish on the gem. Any wish in the world. Robert knew what his wish would be. He wanted his wife back, but that was impossible. He can't wish on a rock. A deep voice echoed in his brain, "Don't do it. You can't bring her back."

Robert decided to give in to his childish desire. Robert clutched the gem for dear life. He closed his eyes and whispered, "I want Julia to come back." Robert opened his eyes. He soon thought of all the stories he's heard of people coming back from the dead. Zombie-like and blood-lust. He quickly closed his eyes again, "I'd prefer it if she wasn't murderous."

He heard a high-pitched scream. This broke him from his trance. He looked up to see a pregnant woman screaming dangling from the rocks. She frantically swung her feet and her fingers began to slip. Robert climbed up quickly to help her. He pulled the woman into his left arm and held on with his right.

He looked at her face, "Julia!" he yelled and a smile grew on his face. "You're here! It worked, oh my, I can't believe it worked!"

"Robby!" Julia yelled, clinging to her husband. "What's happening? Where are we?!" She held on intensely.

"Julia, you'll be safe. I won't let you fall, I promise. You'll be okay. Just put your feet in those holes and your right hand in that crevasse." He held his wife tightly offering support.
He screamed, "Help!" frantically and repeatedly. Nobody came to their rescue. Robert started to scream heavy curses and insults. He questioned the crowd's sanity. Have they gone mad? Why weren't they helping his wife?

"Julia, darling, don't panic and listen. I will get you and our baby out of this safely and we'll have a fabulous life together, but you're going to have to climb."

Robert showed his wife slowly how to do it. She slowly followed. They began to progress their way up the mountain supporting each other.

Robert started to feel comfortable with his wife climbing. He stopped holding onto her and worked on his climbing.

Another scream pierced Robert's ears. He looked to see Julia's hands had slipped on some moss. Her body dangled with nothing but her arm holding on.

He grabbed her hand quickly though he could feel her slipping. She started to slip away for the second time in his life. Her fingers slipped through his.

Robert envisioned the event in slow motion. He saw everything and felt pain every second. He saw her hit the ground.

He screamed in pain; a pain he felt in his heart. He couldn't breathe. His heart raced. He wasn't going to keep going. He let go and felt his body start to fall.

The media was quick to report his death. People around the world knew the story of the man who'd gone insane. Within an hour, a news report came out that captivated the audience.

The anchor sat, hunched over reading the script. In a voice of sorrow, he said, "Beloved free soloist Robert Clinton has passed away. Investigations confirmed that the time of death was 12:53pm, one body found."

# Ignored, but not by choice
By Alondra Rodriguez Rosales

The young girl laid in her month-old castle of blankets and pillows. In a soft haven of pillows, blankets, and her mother's old shirts, she was not just a girl, but a princess. When the enraged cries of her Mama and Papa threatened to envelop her, she hid in the cozy, familiar comforts of a less consuming world.

She decided it was time to go out and play. She wondered if her Mama would be angry that she came back so late. When she finally grew tired of ruling over the few stuffed subjects of her pillow kingdom, she stood and made her way out the door, making sure to grab her stuffed companion Mr. Panda to take along on her journey. She paused before fully leaving though, realizing she had forgotten something.

Anytime she went out to venture off outside and play on her own, she would always inform her Mama of her departure. Of course, she didn't really care. At times the girl wondered if her mother would even realize she was gone if she went a day without telling her. Every time she notified her mother of her leave she was met with no response, left ignored. Despite this, the young girl did not resent her mother, after all the naive eyes of a child are much more forgiving. She decided to find her Mama to talk to her.

"Mama!" Her small voice called out, "Are you here? Mama?"

She was met with no response. There was an odd silence inside her house. It was usually quiet but something felt off. She made sure to check every room. The messy kitchen with dirty dishes laid on just about every surface. Her Mama's room had piles of clothing scattered everywhere, and even in the dirty bathroom. Her Mama was nowhere to be seen. She decided to check out-

side. Perhaps she could find her Papa and then he could help her look. She slipped on a coat to protect her from the autumn cold and put on her worn-out shoes. The little girl ran out the front door. She saw her Mama, and she was crying.

Her face was full of tears and all red and puffy. This wasn't a very unusual sight, as the young girl was used to seeing her mother turn into an emotional mess when intoxicated (which was usually most of the time). A man in a cop uniform stood next to her. He might've been saying something but she was too busy focusing on her Mama to care.

"Mama, what happened? Are you okay? ...Mama? Did I do something wrong again? I'm sorry." Her Mama wouldn't look at her. She was ignoring her except this time was different. Most of the time she was met with at least a glance or some form of acknowledgment. She didn't know if she had done something wrong, if she hadn't been good enough, or if she had somehow let her Mama down.

"Mama I'm sorry. I don't know what I did wrong... Mommy, please don't ignore me... Please, I'm sorry." Her voice was shaky and got all pitchy as she begged her mother. Tears now streamed across her small face that had now also turned puffy and red. Snot ran down her face and she tried to wipe it off with her sleeve. She then noticed the flashing red and blue lights of the police car parked in the street. She wasn't sure why they were even there.

Her question was answered when she got closer to the road. There, laid a small body covered in a white sheet, tire tracks could be seen on the road and she could make out a wrecked car in the distance. An accident had occurred. Upon further inspection of the sheet, familiar short hair could be seen peeking out from under it. A hand of the body held an extremely familiar object, her panda, Mr. Panda. The realization hit; that was her body.

She was dead.

She looked back at the weeping face of her Mama. She would always inform her Mama whenever she would leave and was always ignored. Now she would have to leave for good and just like all the times before, her Mama wouldn't be able to hear her. This was the time it mattered most. She walked over next to her Mama and looked up at her, and just like all the times before she informed her Mama that she was going.

"Mama, I'm gonna have to leave again. I'm sorry this happened, but I think you'll be able to do fine on your own. I just thought I should tell you I was leaving..." She trailed off and walked ahead. Her mother didn't say anything to her. The young girl was ignored once again, except this was the one time her mother hadn't done it on purpose; the one time it wasn't by choice.

## Beneath the Surface
Siena Ridolfo

Elaine broke through the clouds. She never knew that flying could be so fun yet so terrifying. She felt alive and scared and powerful and weak. It was surreal. She was happier than she had ever been. Until she saw something. A flicker of black to her left. She decided to ignore it. It was nothing, she told herself. Until she saw it again, this time in front of her. It looked like smoke and light at the same time. It began to envelop her, cloaking the sunny sky with darkness.

She started to plummet, fast. She didn't know if there was a ground beneath her, a body of water, or just pure nothing. Until she came to a halt. She became aware of a salty smell. Like the ocean.

She again fell for what seemed like hours, but in reality, were only seconds. Then she felt the cold embrace of water enrapture her as she crashed through the surface of the water. She tumbled and thrashed beneath the water. She didn't know what to do. She couldn't breathe. She couldn't see. She could only hear her muffled screams and feel the cold water seeping into her.

Okay. Elaine. Calm down. Slow your heart rate, She thought to herself. She started to float upwards, relief falling over her as she felt cool air sting her face.

And then she realized, oh, she realized, she was in the middle of nowhere in the middle of an ocean and she could not see below the water. Something brushed against her leg. It felt rough and she could feel the salt water stinging where the thing had scratched her. Something bit down on her ankle. She let out a scream of terror as she was pulled under the water. She struggled and struggled trying to be released from the beast's jaws.

In her attempt to escape, she felt a flat spike on the top of the thing's body. Oh god… It was a shark. She felt like she was going to pass out, die, maybe even explode. Until she felt a calm breeze on her foot. What on earth? Then her whole lower half. And then her face. She looked up and was blinded by the sun. She looked down at the ground where she stood and saw green grass in the place of salty water. Strange….

She stared up at the sky as clouds began to form. The blue sky was almost gone by the time she saw a cloud dip down from the blanket of gray. It lengthened and widened and then it touched the ground. She realized she was being tugged towards it, the wind whipping her hair around. By the time she realized what was happening, it was too late. She was lifted up off of the ground and sped towards the tornado. Around and around and around she went, her arms and legs flying about.

She felt like she was going to pass out, she could feel her blood pressure dropping. And then the tornado was gone. She was suspended mid-air, instead of falling as she had expected. And again she began plummeting. She couldn't see the ground beneath her. She felt like she was going to fall forever, never to touch solid earth again. Then she saw green, grassy mountains speeding towards her. She was about to land, she was about to die, her bones shattered on impact.

And then she didn't.

She awoke in a cold sweat, breathing heavy and fast. She felt dizzy and very overheated. She threw off her layers of warm winter blankets and sheets and ran through her little cottage. She began to weep at the sight of her late son's drawing he had

made when he was four, some thirty years ago. Martin, her son, her everything, had been lost at sea for years. She had given up hope long ago.

Next to the drawing were pictures of her hometown. There had been a tornado when she was nine that had taken her mother and her little sister, Emma. She stared out at the open mountains her cottage overlooked where her husband, Percy, had plummeted to his death. She walked over, pushed open the window, and breathed in the fresh, early morning air. She let the light breeze tassel her hair. She took in the sweeping mountains, the jagged pikes, the sun rising just above the mountains. She felt herself sway.

She leaned even further out of the window, closing her eyes. She couldn't live with all of her loss. She had dealt with the pain for so long, the burden of being alone, the feeling of complete uselessness. She felt herself lose balance. Elaine fell out of the window. She let it happen.

# The Woman I Married
By Audrey Shockley

Jonathan and his wife Ashley were standing outside their car. The cool mountain breeze blew his dark brown hair back. The couple were on their way to a retreat and were filling up their car with gas, the smell Jonathan had always hated. Jonathan Whitlock was 26 and his wife of 2 years was 24. Jonathan was currently in the prime of his life. 6'5", muscular, and a fabulous career in basketball. He was a household name but not for being a good basketball player.

It was for his horrible acts of sportsmanship and his anger. The way he cursed at his wife from the court, and the taunts. The physical encounters with opponents in the locker rooms didn't help. The couple got into the car. His wife was driving. They sat in dead silence, like the woods at night. A few minutes later, Jonathan's phone rang. The name Ella Katz appeared on his phone.

"Who is that dear?" Ashley asked, concentrating on the road. "Ella," The man opened his gum and put a piece in his mouth.

"My sister?" Ashley sped up the car. Her foot pressed against the gas pedal slightly harder.

"Yes, and darling please slow down the car. What are you trying to do, kill us both?" The man slightly chuckled at his own statement. He picked up his cold phone and pressed the green button, "Hello? This is Jonathan speaking."

"Yes hello, Jonathan. I have something to tell you," Ella said, her voice cutting off slightly. She sounded urgent. Jonathan kept quiet to let her speak, "Your wife is cheating on you."

Before he had the chance to respond, He felt his body be jolted forward into a soft cushion. The phone slipped out of his hand. His gum shot to the back of his throat. His face was suffocating in the bag protecting him. He could feel his world spinning as the car tumbled down the side of the hill. His heavy body was being tossed around like a feather, the only thing saving him being his seatbelt. The car kept tumbling and all of the sudden he felt one jolt pushing him further into the airbag and he heard the sound of the window breaking.

He reached out suddenly for the door handle. He pulled slightly and it opened. His body fell out of the car onto the dirt. He crawled under a tree and sat there for a few minutes. He struggled to keep his eyes open and everything was dizzy, but he rested. His mind was blank as he laid against the hard uncomfortable roots and trees. He threw his head back and used it as a pillow and he ran his fingers through the soft dirt. In a matter of minutes, the man had collected himself and stood up.

He stumbled over to the other side of the car and saw Ashley lying on the ground. "Give me your phone," Jonathan spoke softly. He wanted to scream but he couldn't.

"Wait, please I can explain," Ashley replied. Suddenly a wave of anger came over Jonathan. "Give me the phone!" He managed to yell. He held out his hand in a demanding manner. Ashley looked away from him and to the ground. She hesitantly pulled her phone out of her pocket and handed it to the man. Jonathan took her phone and unlocked it. He looked through her contacts but noticed a strange amount of text messages to Jonathan's best friend, Will. He had been friends with him since high school. They spent so much time with each other. He was like a brother to him. He opened these texts and saw thousands of messages. Heart emojis, I love you's, flirting. Tears formed in his eyes. He began to cry until he saw one message.

"Once he dies, I'll get his money. I've been slipping pills into his drink to speed up the process. lol." The text read. Jonathan stared at that one message for a long time. His mind was blank. He stood, saying nothing, doing nothing. Then suddenly he started slamming the phone into the tree. He did this over, and over, and over again. He was a raging bull. The phone shattered in his hands and he tossed it to the ground. His wife watched, her mouth wide open. He clenched his fists and looked at her, trying to restrain herself.

"How will we call for help," she asked. Jonathan rolled his eyes at the dumb question, "We'll use my phone obviously." He walked over to the car. He saw his phone, also shattered. He slammed his fist into the car door. He winced in pain at his own action and took a deep breath. "Jonathan," Ashley said weakly, "What are we going to do?" Jonathan looked at the setting sun. "Build shelter I guess. Also, start a fire." He rubbed his chin and looked around. He ordered Ashley to gather wood and leaves. Later, Ashley brought back materials. Jonathan built a shelter and fire. The large man slumped back on the rock as soon as he got the fire going. He felt weak at that moment. His body was in pain. His wife didn't love him. They were stuck in the woods with no help.

"Jonathan," Ashley glanced at him before quickly looking back at the floor. He looked back at her. He couldn't reply without crying. So he sat quiet waiting for her to say something. "I'm sorry," she muttered. Jonathan could see the tears in her eyes. It was completely dark other than the fire but he could see the reflection of the light. He sighed.

"It's," He paused, looking for the right words. "It's not okay, and I will turn you in after this, but I will make sure we both make it out of this alive." Ashley nodded, still looking at the ground.

"You don't seem mad. I thought you'd be more angry. I was scared of you," Ashley said. She fidgeted with her hands. Jonathan looked up at the stars. "Me too," he said

He found himself oddly calm. He was mad but also at peace. He was mad at Ashley but he didn't have the strength to fight with her about it anymore. He just wanted to sleep it off and have it all be a bad dream. He let out a heavy sigh and laid against the tree. He started humming to himself a nice peaceful song his mom used to sing to him. It made him feel warm.
"I don't love you, but one thing I've always admired about you is how smart you are," she said. Jonathan kept a straight face trying to remain emotionless. "So how will people find us?" The wonderful smell of burning firewood filled the air.

"Somebody must've seen the accident. If they didn't, well, that's part of what this fire is for" He pointed to the fire, proud of the large flame he created. "Why don't you go fetch us some granola bars? They are in the glove compartment, if you can't, don't worry about it. Don't hurt yourself by getting something we don't need right now."

Ashley limped off, still injured by the car accident. At that moment Jonathan heard something in the distance. The wonderful sound of a helicopter. He stood up quickly, on the tip of his toes. He waved his arms and the glaring light.

"Sir," The loud official on the megaphone said, "We are sending down a rope. Please gather any other survivors." Then suddenly he heard Ashley shriek. He ran over and saw her on the ground. She was bleeding out. He ran over and collapsed to his knees beside her.
"Ashley! Darling!" He yelled. He looked at his wife on the ground. She was limp and bleeding from her abdomen. She had a giant wound that hadn't been there before. He looked

back up at the helicopter coming closer to them. He started to feel dizzy, the pain of the wreck finally affecting him. His eyes started to feel heavy but he knew he couldn't rest. He couldn't rest because of Ashley.

He scurried on the ground over to the car and climbed in the back seat. He took two towels they had packed and a few water bottles and crawled back over to her. He sat her up against a tree root and began dabbing her wounds with the wet towel. He realized she was wearing gloves when she wasn't before. Then he saw a knife with blood. He felt worse and his body was failing. He reached for the knife and finally grabbed it by the handle. Right as he did his eyes closed and his world went dark.

He woke up in the rescue helicopter. Three armed men rushed to him and placed him in handcuffs. Then he realized. He'd been framed. He realized this was still the same woman who wanted to kill him. He realized she hadn't changed and he was foolish to think she did after just a few hours.

"Mr. Whitlock, You're under arrest for the attempted murder of Ashley Whitlock and assault with a weapon. You have the right to remain silent. If you don't have a lawyer you will be provided one."

## Stories Heard from Latinos
By Edwin Bastida Villa & Diego Rangel

Up above
From a far land
It seemed there was
To be a plan

From far seas
To large lands
There's more to expand
Rich lives and scarce lives

It looked like it was paradise
For whom to wonder bright lives
As the sun so they can thrive
New life plans are to come
As we seek and strum

From the lands up above
There was a new life to come
From stories heard
From up above
From up above

**Alluring Almond Amber Eyes**
By Ryan Hayes

I sit cold yet still here
With not an ounce of fear
Stone cold
In your immaculate hold

A fine creation
A beautiful variation
Of what I wish to be
So you see

You are a picture with no filter
Like a soft, fluttering, cold, snow from winter
So stunning its cunning
But yet no one is running
                                    To you

Bad?
No, not even sad
Your soft almond amber eyes
Entice me with no despise
Of what might come

I'm not numb
To your trap
One I'm all to willing to unwrap

Because although those evil amber eyes
Hold something I can't compromise
The fiery love within me
Will never be lost at sea

**To my friends**
By Alana Cortes

Sitting in a classroom
Or anywhere, really
Thinking to yourself...

    *Existence is meaningless*

        *People are stupid*

            *We're all just waiting for death*

        And yet...

            Just maybe...

Your mind begins to

    d    r    i    f    t

To slightly less
morbid
things

A little better for your mental health
Or perspective of life
You might glance across the room
Or over a memory
Thinking fondly of the times to come
Or ones that have already passed

It's nice to have friends

        I should make some.

**Why I Dislike My Job**
By Josh Nielsen

So close to the weekend, yet so far away
I sit in my seat and type, to my dismay
Wondering when I'm leaving
I work late into the evening
Eating little to none
Because there is no time for fun
When I get home I fall asleep exhausted
It's the only time when work is halted
Work is the one place I dread.
I no longer remember the words of advice my coworkers said.

**One Day**
By Sadie Vukoder-Ash

One day, I
will be able to be
proud of myself
for everything I
have accomplished.
One day, I
will be able to look in the mirror,
happy with how I look.
One day
maybe tomorrow,
maybe in a decade.
Eventually, I
hope that one day
all my troubles and struggles
see their way through.
One day,
all of this will come true.
Until then, I
will remain
unconfident,
and insecure.
But I
know that my day
is coming soon.
One day I
will feel secure
and confident.
Probably not today,
but my day
is gonna come

One day.

**Nuclear Life**
By Ansley Peace

2 houses 2 homes
2 kitchens 2 phones
2 couches where I lay
2 places that I stay
Moving moving from here and there
Monday to friday I'm everywhere
Don't get me wrong it's not that bad
But often times it makes me sad
I just want to live that nuclear life.

**Jealousy**
By Alejandra Zepeda-Zelaya

I saw that pretty girl again
With her long beautiful hair
I always get compared to her
I wish I looked like her
She has it all
a nice house
and cool parents
She has the prettiest eyes
They are a light ocean blue
No wonder everyone likes her
While I have short hair
and deep chocolate eyes
I just wish I was her
She's got all A's while
I have B's and C's
The way people talk about her
just bring an anger in me
But I still want to be her
What is this feeling I feel?
Is it anger or sadness?

No.


It's my jealousy that haunts me

**Happy Diwali**
By Siri Vanmali

We celebrate the powerful force of good over evil.
We celebrate Diwali known as: Festival of lights.
We celebrate Diwali for five full days.
We celebrate by lighting bright diyas.
We celebrate a Hindu holiday.
We celebrate our siblings.
We celebrate you,
Love you,
Diwali.

**Hang in there!**
By Emery Jorgensen

What in the- who's there!?
Well, good morning to you too.
Hmm? Should I know you?

Let's get on with it.
You came for some grand ballad.
Am I not wrong, no?

I have bad news then.
Nothing that meaningful here.
You can leave. Go on.

Aww, why the long face?
Go read Shakespeare or something.
Heard he's uplifting.

You're still here? Really?
Why do you do this to me . . .
Not leaving, huh? Fine.

"You've made it this far,
Must be doing something right.
Probably, at least."

Not bad. Happy now?
Kind of inspiring, I guess.
I kind of like it.

**Home**
By Alejandra Zepeda-Zelaya

Where is home?
Is home where your parents are?
Or is home with your friends?
Could home be made of sticks and mud?

Is your home 20 feet tall
Or is your home 5 inches small?
Home is not a place with games
Nor is it a place full of money

Home is where your glory and success it at
Home is our space we can feel comfortable

It can be your atmosphere to share anything
We live and learn to return to our home
Home is where we feel most comfortable
That is what we call a home

**We are all equal**
by Tarahji Anderson

We need to treat others equal
So we can all be good people
We don't want a 2020 sequel

We need to treat people fair
To show that we care
Or we'll start another a global flare

We need to treat others
Like we treat ourselves
We should put our prejudices up on the shelves

So let's all be grateful for who we are
Let's all shine bright like a star
Or we will never know who we really are

**Deep**
By Andrew Harson

How must you fit in
If even in the deepest places
You are just an outcast
Lost in the thoughts
Of things unexplainable
Hidden in the deepest areas of the mind
Stowed away

The people of this earth
Don't realize how much
A simple word
A simple action
A simple thought
Could put you even deeper into the mind

And if you slip up
You could get lost
In the deep

**I Dream**
By Dominick Prietti

I dream of a world where joy
And happiness
Will shine like a pearl,
All mankind will stop sapping the soul
God will climb down to bless this world,
Wretchedness will be no such thing upon this world I dream.

**A Shade of Power**
By Alex Smith

The shade of my skin may be seen as dim,
Just a simple reflection of what my ancestors used to be.
It may even be viewed as a weakness,
But in reality it's my power.

The strength, the determination,
The perseverance my skin holds
The story it tells, from scars, to marks,
And simply just the color

The impact of my skin is powerful,
The power my actions hold,
Simply because my skin reflects
Every person similar to me.

The upbringing of a young black man,
Some may fear the potential
And power he holds.

The upbringing of a young black woman,
Some may fear her intelligence,
And the power she also holds

People claim that the world is equal now,
And everyone is treated with equality.
But is this really true?

They try to water down the power my skin inherits,
But they don't come near success and never will
Such power cant be taken away, only utilized.
The color of my skin is a symbol for strength
The impact of my skin is powerful

## The Locket
By Jorja Holmes

By Jorja Holmes

The farm was beautiful, it really was, but Jemma still found it peculiar. It was hard not to when there was no wind and no birds in the sky. And the wall. There was a large, eerie stone wall surrounding the plain fields of her Aunt's farm. It was growing covered in moss, and vines were growing from in between the bricks. When Jemma had arrived, she asked about it.

"You will not go outside."

"Why?" Jemma had asked, truly curious.

"You will not leave the wall. It is not safe." And that was the end of the conversation. It wasn't worth it to argue anyway, she had nowhere else to go with her parents overseas.

Jemma didn't listen. She had done everything there was to do in this boring place; ridden the horses, brushed them, fed the cows and other animals. And now she was bored.

She was just walking; Aunt Phoebe couldn't get angry with her. She had warned her not to go outside the wall. She had never said anything about touching it. She continued her stroll, the still air warm around her.

She hiked up her skirts with her free hand, to not trip in the tall, un-mowed grass. It was peaceful being so far away from civilization. No people bothering her, no men asking for her hand though she was already betrothed. She enjoyed it out here. She wanted to stay forever, but she knew it wasn't possible.

Her soon-to-be husband would never allow it. She was to be a housewife, bear children, and cook meals. And that was all she would ever be, in the eyes of the people.

But she wanted more.

She wanted more than getting on her knees and scrubbing floors, listening to her husband without question, bearing him as many children as he wished.

Jemma wanted to be free.

Lost in her head, she almost didn't notice when her finger got caught on a slim chain in the rock. Jemma tilted her head. Looking at it, she found it wrapped paranormally around her finger. Strange.

She dropped her skirts, grabbed the chain with her right hand, and yanked. The force of it threw her to the ground. She could only pray that her new dress skirts weren't grass stained. Aunt Phoebe would eat her alive.

Catching her breath, she looked down at the mysterious chain. It was a slim, silver heart-shaped locket. Despite being stuck in stone for god knows how long, it was warm to the touch like it had a strange aura to it.

"Huh," Jemma mumbled to herself and held the locket tight in her palm. It felt large and heavy, but Jemma couldn't figure out why. Was she weakened from the fall?

Clearly, she was, because she was beginning to hear a whisper, seemingly from inside the locket.

Slowly, making sure she had the locket secure in her hand, she stood. Should she open it? Should she throw it into the grass?

Her curiosity outweighed her rationality and she opened the clasp.

Little did she know, it would be the best mistake she ever made.

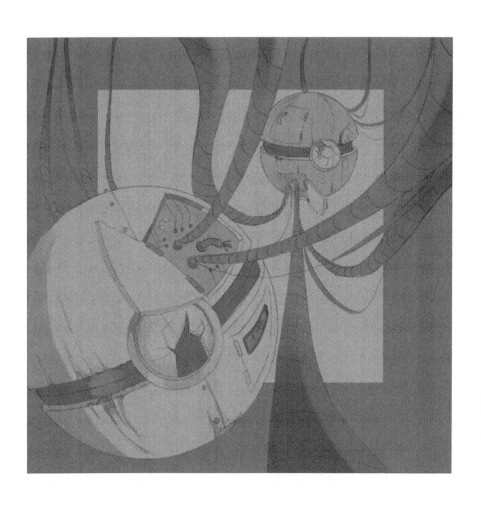

# Invaded
By Anouk Bridges

Frances Spade was a minimalistic person who didn't like to dwell too much on his past. In fact, he didn't ever want his past brought up. His parents were taken away by strange individuals when he was just five years old. As a result, he was bounced between several foster homes. He usually kept quiet, just focusing on his work behind the register at the cluttered magic shop in his small city. The magic shop wasn't visited often since most people were more occupied with the newer technologies of his generation. His only true friend was Eden Archer. Eden was his polar opposite. She was excited and peppy everyday.

"Heya, Franky!" Eden shouted as she busted through the door of his shop. She gave him the nickname "Franky" when they first became friends and she's just used it ever since. "Hi." He managed a little wave. While he didn't understand how she always had this happy attitude, he needed it in his life.

As Frances was walking home from work one evening, he heard a ding! coming from his phone. He assumed it was Eden so he rushed it out of his pocket. The message was addressed to someone with a completely different name than him. It read,"Hello, Delula Forger. We have heard of your great combat skills and would like to welcome you into our agency. Our job is to terminate any and all cyborgs from our city. Please consider."

Baffled, Frances replied simply stating they had messaged the wrong individual and told them who he was. They quickly replied, "Apologies for the inconvenience. Due to our security measures you must join our agency or you will be terminated within the next hour." Confused and scared, he felt he had no choice but to agree. Frances woke up the next day to the sound of tap tap tap repeating on his door. He jumped out of bed, disheveled and half-dressed.

"I'm coming!" Frances shouted from his room, frantically stumbling to the front of his scarcely decorated apartment. He reached the door and pressed the fingerprint unlocking system. The door slid open to reveal three people dressed in suits, heavily armed.

"May I help you?" He questioned as they held still.

"You're coming with us. Pack your things." One lady said in a monotone voice.

He didn't waste another second, scared of what they could do to him if he didn't do what they said. He trudged past a few unfinished and discarded inventions left on his desk and rummaged through his drawers. After a few minutes, he arrived back at the front door, an older model, red Suitcase 3000 reluctantly wheeling behind him. The people appeared to have not moved more than an inch. They seemed to talk into a small microphone embedded in their clothing. Once he had appeared in the doorway, they ceased their conversation and began marching away leaving Frances to follow quickly behind.

"Do you know of a girl by the name of Eden Archer?" One of the individuals asked.

"I do."

"She's been captured. Your first mission is to find her."

"She-- wait, what?"

"She has been captured."

Frances followed them still but slowed his pace. He kept his eyes on his own feet as he felt his heart drop to his stomach.

After walking the entire way to avoid being spotted by cyborgs, Frances and the agents reached a bunker-like building. He walked through the big underground doorway to a large lobby filled with gadgets. It was like his apartment: quite dull and filled with unfinished projects. Frances didn't get enough time to look as he was ushered forward.

"Your training begins now." A lot happened in the two weeks he trained with the agents. The woman they had intended to hire had been brought in after successfully reaching her. Delula was her name and he envied her a bit.

"I can't do it!" Frances shouted after being struck to the ground by a training bot. The agents tasked Delula with the job to collect information about Eden's whereabouts and she was great at her job. Frances begged and pleaded to be given this mission, but was denied each time. They said it was too dangerous for the level of action required.

He eventually snuck out and took whatever gadgets he could find lying around. Once he'd reached the presumed headquarters of the cyborgs, it was a piece of cake. He was weary of the simplicity of breaking in. He was soon met with several guards, but easily wiped them out with a few blasts from one of the attachable wrist lasers. Upon defeating them, he was filled with false confidence. He came upon a larger room with cells upon cells of humans. There were guards everywhere. He almost turned heel and ran, but a pair of familiar faces stopped Frances in his tracks.

"Mom…? Dad?" His parents were staring at him, pointing a laser to his face with somber eyes as if they were being forced.

He hadn't seen them in 18 years but he hadn't much time to think. He ducked quickly and ran after them both. He didn't want to do them any harm so he threw the netting that he had tied to his waist. Miraculously, it did the job. He wanted to stay. He really did, but he had to find Eden. Frances desperately looked around the cell block until he landed on the face he'd recognize anywhere.

"Eden!"

He bolted toward her. She was fine but the metal bars on her cell were difficult to get through. He was being bombarded by several other guards and the urge to leave Eden behind was tempting. His arms hurt and so did his legs. He felt like his limbs would fall off. He tried one final time to bust through the bars. This time, he succeeded.

"Eden! You're safe now…"

"I-- how did you get in here?"

"It's a long story. I'll tell you later."

The guards were relentless, and began attacking again but he couldn't give up, not on his friend. His only friend. Frances continued fighting off the guards, waving Eden ahead, urging her to leave. She hesitated before sprinting away as fast as she could. Her legs were sore from sitting in her cramped cell for two weeks.

It soon became clear Frances was taking a while to catch up to her. She stopped in her tracks and sprinted in the direction she had come from. She bumped into a guard, but before she could react, the guard collapsed to the ground. Frances was running toward her. He looked as worn and beaten as the old suitcase that followed him to training.

"Frances?"

"Eden. Listen to me now. You need to get out of here immediately"

"But what about you?"

"I'll be fine, just go. Take this with you." Frances pushed his best laser gun into her palm. Eden gave him a long look before reluctantly charging through several hallways until she came across a small hatch door. She made it. She was greeted by several agents armed from head to toe and she jumped back upon seeing them, nearly falling.

"Don't hurt me!" She put her hands up in front of her and the agents lowered their weapons. Eden exhaled and sank to the floor, sobbing.

"Frances told me to go.. A-and I.. HE'S NOT BACK!" She wailed. The agents didn't respond to her cries; instead, they began speaking into their microphones. KLANG! A loud bang was heard from under the hatch door. Eden ran to the hatch before the agents could stop her. There she found Frances, beaten and dead. Eden's face showed no expression as she trudged toward safety, leaving the agents to finish what Frances started.

**Getting older**
By Alejandra Zepeda-Zelaya

I remember when I was 5
Riding on my first bike with my friends
Having nothing to do
Kids were nice to everyone
Then I started getting older

At 7 years old I had to do more work
Some kids were big jerks
Once I turned 10
I had teachers on top of me
Just to finish one piece of paper
People started to get meaner
It started to get rough

Then I was about to turn 12
I still have a lot of work to do
People didn't change how mean they are
Didn't have enough time to get with friends
I wish I was 5 again.

**Life is a Beauty**
By Haven Dendy

Life is a beauty
but all around the world,
every second someone is getting
harmed, beaten, or even murdered.

And you're in your house
playing a game while
someone is getting beaten.

Be grateful for what you've got.
Man, I had to learn that fast.
I lost my 2 uncles
before I got to meet them.

It's the same
All over the world
So lets say in Brazil
Someone is losing
a brother
a dad
a sister
or a mother

Live life and love it.
The only thing that can stop you is death,
so just live life, man.

**A Peaceful Slumber**
By Treasure Williams

An escape from reality has been completed,
Now that I've served my time, let it be meaningful,
And it be known, I have finally retreated:
My self-awareness promptly roaming free,
Letting my imagination work in authority,
Enchanting my head with old debris,
That become a temporary priority:
As the sun trades places with the moon,
The birds break in song,
A return back to reality is now in abloom,
And set to begin strong:

I think of this new day now like a blank canvas,
Ready to receive my grandness.

**Mama's Perfumes**
by Anouk Bridges

My mom has a box
Big for super small bottles
So many to choose

Most sweetly scented,
others that like to bite back,
but all so cherished

They bring her such joy
That's why I love borrowing
my mama's perfumes

## Friend, Friend
By Honesti McKinney-Sullivan

Friend, friend, what is a friend?
You talking about a friend that puts you down?
No, that's not a friend!

Friend, friend, What is a friend?
You talking about a friend that you trust
Trust with all your personal business
And then they told everyone?
No, that's not a friend!

Friend, friend, what is a friend?
You talking about a friend that changes
Changes on you when someone else comes?
No, that's not a friend!

Friend, friend, what is a friend?
You talking about a friend that abuses
Abuses you and calling you names that you do not like?
No, that's not a friend!

Friend, friend, what is a friend?
You talking about a friend that is toxic
Toxic towards you and makes you uncomfortable
NO,NO, NO, NO, NO that's not a friend!

So friend, friend, what is a friend
and what are they for?

# The Four: Eris' finger
By Anouk Bridges

It was the year 2173 in a nation ruled by four gods; Isocrates: the god of peace, Eris: the goddess of envy, Asante: the god of gratitude, and lastly, Capaneus: the god of corruption. Their nation was quite orderly despite the gods' complete differences.

In a sense, they balanced each other. Except when it came to Capaneus' complaining, they were the best of friends, having tea together every Wednesday unless their duties prevented them. Each god was assigned a portion of the nation to look over but there were no defined borders to contain the citizens; everyone went about their business and looked after themselves. The gods were mere trophies, cast aside on a dusty shelf. Their "duties" consisted of visiting villages to reassure the citizens with their presence, little as they cared.

Though the gods were the divine rulers, the citizens decided laws and organized their own lists of common knowledge. Sometimes the gods didn't care, since it meant less work, but Eris stayed jealous of the citizens for this and that reason, and Isocrates was always calming her down. Capaneus was full of himself and wondered why they didn't pay attention or consult the four of them. Meanwhile, Asante felt lucky for the extra free time.

"Ugh! Such imbeciles down there.." Capaneus muttered under his breath.

"'Calm down. It's not so bad," Isocrates soothed.

"We barely ask much of them and they can't even turn a glance our way? Tsk-"

"Quiet down Capaneus. Complaining isn't going to do anything."

Capaneus continued his rant to Isocrates while the other two gods were off somewhere else. On a picnic, they were. They'd finished eating already and were now playing a game. The pair got along quite well so they'd often sneak away to chat or have a little childish game when Capaneus bickered with Isocrates. Isocrates didn't dare argue back. Asante typically won each game causing Eris to become a little jealous and desperately challenge him to another game. She was determined to win.

"Why do you always have to win? I wish I could be like you." Eris crossed her arms with a pouty expression laid across her face.

"Hah, I'm glad luck is on my side."

"There's no way you win with just sheer luck, you cheater!"

He gave her a pat on the back. "Let's head back, shall we?" He took her by the hand and she sighed as her body relaxed. They headed back to their home up in the stars where they could watch over the nation. Reluctant to come back to Capaneus' bickering, Asante and Eris braced themselves, but what they came back to was a surprise. Isocrates and Capaneus weren't there. No trace. Nothing.

It didn't matter how much they searched, they simply couldn't find a clue as to their whereabouts. They looked down at their nation to find a chunk of it drifting away. Shocked, Eris and Asante agreed to inspect the situation. Asante went to the chunk, and Eris checked on the rest of the nation. The citizens were in a panic. Hundreds of homes were torn in half, leaving thousands homeless. Asante found Isocrates hovering in the clouds above the drifting chunk of the nation. He seemed unphased, simply watching the hysteria down below.

"Isocrates? What on earth happened?" Asante hurried to him with nothing but concern in his gentle eyes.

"I've decided to take this portion of our nation for myself if Capaneus is going to be so unreasonable."

"What happened between you two?"

"Well, listen close dear Asante."

Isocrates told him what happened, beginning with the moment he and Eris left. Capaneus had continued his bickering with Isocrates, becoming progressively louder. He'd had enough of Capaneus' shouting so he silenced him.

"Capaneus! That's enough. I've heard enough of your complaints and constant brags."

"Oh, of course. Mr. Goody-two-shoes can't stand for someone to be upset." He threw his hands up in the air, "You never want to hear anything I have to say. Is it so hard to lend an ear?"
"I just prefer to not witness anyone being this angered. Take a breath."

Capaneus could not see the harm in venting to what he assumed was a friend. He didn't know how he was doing anything wrong and he stormed away. In Isocrates' eyes, Capaneus' constant resentment of their citizens was something that could easily lead to war between the gods and humans.

It wasn't just this particular argument that had caused Isocrates to go so far as to split away his land. He couldn't stand a friendship with Capaneus if it meant constant bickering. It was too much.

"Hm. Capaneus is such a pain sometimes. I'm grateful at least someone has the sense to put him in his place."

"I can't believe I've broken the peace over this." Isocrates rubbed his forehead, disappointed in himself. "Oh, what have I done..."

"It's alright! Don't worry so much. Why don't I join my quarter of the nation with yours? We shall invite Eris. That thing can rule his own nation"

Isocrates nodded and Asante went to his quarter. He held out a hand, materializing a staff decorated in gold so shiny it hurt to lay eyes upon. It had a marbled gem at the top that rotated slowly. Asante drove it into the ground with a crack of lightning and the land split in two. The hysteria reached a crescendo. The humans were scrambling and, once again, several became homeless or jobless because of the gods' reckless division.

Asante led his chunk of land towards Isocrates' portion, creating large waves that knocked against its sides. He matched it up with Isocrates' land as if it were nothing but a puzzle piece. He placed a hand on his hip and snapped his staff into oblivion.

"Thank you for your help," he said to the staff as it morphed into pixelated shapes until it vanished. He made a point to show his gratitude whenever he used it.

Meanwhile, Eris was having a chat with Capaneus. At about the same time Asante had reached Isocrates earlier, Eris had reached Capaneus. He had been sitting in the clouds, arms crossed, in a mood. Eris caught sight of him and called out.

Capaneus scoffed and lifted his chin, barely glancing at her. She went to him and placed a hand on his back.

"What happened?"

"Psh, would you actually even listen, unlike that imbecile?"

"Yes of course. I'm all ears."

Capaneus told the same story, though he sugar-coated his actions. Eris had some sympathy for him after he'd told his version of the story. Her sympathy became more than just comforting. After a short while of convincing, Eris agreed to side with him. She couldn't wait to ask Asante to join them, but any hope was lost when she looked down to see his assigned portion joined with Isocrates'. She was baffled that he was siding with Isocrates. Her displeasure was written all over her face.

"Eris, leave him be. It's fine. We don't need him." He held onto her wrist.

"But he's my friend! I can't just let that dishonorable idiot deceive him!" She pulled her wrist free and hurried as quickly as possible to Asante, dipping below the clouds.

She called out to him once she was within hearing distance. Asante perked up and looked for the direction of her familiar voice. His smile quickly faded upon seeing her expression. He saw that angered face and it troubled him. "Eris, come down here!" He called. She soared down to his level and lashed out at Asante, paying no mind to Isocrates.

"How could you choose him?!" She jabbed her finger into the middle of his chest.

"Ow- Eris! You know that hurts me. You need to calm yourself. It's not the end of the world. Why are you acting like he's the bad one?"

"Because he is, and you're an idiot for believing him."

Her words hurt him. It was as if a knife pierced his heart. What friendship Eris and Asante had was a tattered rope now, hanging by a single thread, ready to collapse. All he could do at the moment was be silent. Eris scoffed at him then crossed the wide span of sea, back to Capaneus. She couldn't explain her jealousy for Isocrates, nor her anger at Asante. All she could do was pick a side, so that's what she did. She chose to rule a nation with Capaneus, a rude and selfish creature, but even worse, she barely knew why.

Throughout the next century, their connections grew further apart. They agreed to build a bridge between the two lands, but it was hardly used. Each side was actually given laws assigned by the gods. The side of Asante and Isocrates was known as Divine. Capaneus and Eris' side was known as Corrupt. Their nation had fallen to ruins. Capaneus had created his own dictatorship with Eris at his side.

The two sides were at war now, driven by hatred and spite. "Shields up! Weapons armed!" Capaneus' voice boomed over the large crowd. Isocrates ordered his soldiers on his side of the land as well. "CHARGE." They both yelled in perfect unison. Their soldiers charged across the bridge. The gods cast a few blasts at the other side's land.

The only sounds that filled the air were the clinks of swords, the yells and cries of soldiers, and the explosions. Clouds cloaked the sky, making the atmosphere even more dark and somber. Something caught Isocrates' eye in the middle of the clashing.

A young boy, sobbing over his mother's corpse. The sight jerked his heart. He was always too wrapped up in his emotions to notice what effects this fighting had on the people. He turned his head back to face Capaneus.

"Capaneus!"

"What now?"

"Maybe… Maybe this fighting should stop and we could go back to being whole."

"Hah! Are you kidding? There's always good and evil. They're destined to war."

"Maybe it doesn't need to be that way though? It's hurting the people."

"This isn't about them."

Isocrates stared down at their lands and all he could see was destruction. Even his side looked nearly as broken as Capaneus' land. Each time he glanced down, his heart sank lower and lower.

The wars went on for decades more. The two lands were crumbling apart. The only citizens left standing grew to despise the gods. They rose up against them, fighting alongside each other. Their shields barely stood a chance against the gods' power, but the decades of fighting had sharpened their skills.

"How can humans withstand this much? Goodness- " Asante wiped his forehead, panting.

"Hah- it's fun! Worthy opponents." Capaneus chuckled with his hands on his hips. He had a psychotic glint in his eyes. "So sick. Just like always."

"What's that supposed to mean!?"

"Well it--" Asante's sentence was cut off. He noticed the humans cheering. For a moment, he was confused then his eyes wandered down. A spear had struck him through the middle of his chest. He thought of Eris' finger--her anger--nearly a century before. His vision blurred, his ears rang. Time froze.

Spring comes and leaves without you

—June

**To the One I Lost**
By Ryan Hayes

To the One I Lost
By Ryan Hayes

I walked out onto the stage not a butterfly in my stomach as I smiled brightly, the lights blaring in my face were almost blinding but I didn't mind.

It made me realize that everyone was here for me. If you couldn't tell at the time, I loved being in the spotlight. The smell of the freshly washed stage, not a mark left on it as my heels, clicked against the wooden planks.

I slowly tucked my sparkling red dress under me as I sat down, the dress I so dearly hated but you loved. I then began to play. I remember the feeling. The feeling of my hands gliding over the piano like a bright summer's day as the leaves gracefully flutter through the sky.

The light notes as my fingertips pressed against the cold keys. The stage was my home.

I know it's sad but it's true. I felt safer here. Funny how things change.

I opened my eyes and I stood there in the green grass that tickled against my ankles. Usually, I'd be smiling from the tickles but I knew it was inappropriate and something inside me just isn't letting me. I couldn't tell if my spring allergies were messing with me or if I really was crying.

I didn't want to cry over her. I don't want to cry over my mom cause she truly was an awful person but she taught me everything I knew about piano.

The spring allergies were still getting to me and I remember wiping my tears with the black sleeve of my dress.

Black, one of my favorite colors, was ruined right at that moment. Black was such a sad color. Why not wear a color that I didn't like to the funeral so it wouldn't be ruined by the overwhelming amount of sadness there, something like hot pink, it might make me vomit but at least I'd have a reason not to be here.

I'll forever remember the day I met you. It was not long after the funeral when I was walking home. My feet were sore from standing and the smallest step made an aching pain crawl up my back.

I remember I was walking along the sidewalk to the park. The park was my favorite place because I got to watch this one guy every day at 11:30 in the morning walk a whole bunch of dogs and absolutely get trampled but of course, you knew that.

It brought joy to me in the toughest days of my life but now I realize I should have at least gone and helped him up.

I didn't have the guts to, but you did. You ran over like the dogs had run over the man. Your curly jet-black hair flew over your bright green eyes, your freckled face was masked in worry for the poor man.

I just watched with a blank face. I probably looked stupid like an old man having a grumpy day because for some reason old people are always grumpy. Strange, you'd think after everything old people have gone through they'd know to treat us better so we don't have to go through that as well.

I had a feeling that if you had the chance to grow up you wouldn't be like the rest of the old people. I mean look at you now, even I could go help the man but didn't. Your hands gently intertwined with his pulling him up from the ground.

At the time I didn't know how your hands felt but now I do, cold yet a sudden warmness always flushes into my heart as I hold them. I wonder if the man felt that warm feeling or if he was too overcome by the coldness of your soft palms.

He seemed overjoyed for sure as your fingers gently lingered over the dog's slick fur like how the blades of grass lingered in the poor man's hair.

You slowly turned to me and I wasn't sure what to do. A soft gasp left my lips. I was afraid you were going to confront me for not helping the dog walker. You were always unpredictable.

I wasn't sure what your reaction was to me looking away but I knew you probably had a look of confusion. I guess it seemed quite unpredictable for you as well. Didn't it? You didn't bother walking over to me. I suppose you had found me strange at the time, but I found you strange as well. That's why every part of my body was begging for you not to come over here.

I heard a sweet sound and before you think of a child's laughter, that is absolutely not true. In fact, I despise children. They are always so hyper and slobber all over the place and don't get me started about babies. If I had a child it probably wouldn't even make it to two years old. They are constantly touching everything and, who knows, maybe I'll accidentally leave out a bottle of acid and it gets into their hands.

The sweet sound was the beautiful melody and soft tone of a violin. It was deep yet peaceful. I turned my head to the noise and there you were. Your tender fingers held the violin as if it were your world. The bow gently nested between your fingers.

I watched as the hair on the bow ran across the slim strings of the violin. Even if I were to cover my ears I felt as if your graceful movements would show exactly what the violin was to sound like.

Your eyes were closed at the time but I suppose you felt me staring at you because your eyes fluttered open. I remember staring into your emerald green eyes for an awkward amount of time before realizing that I had been staring.

My slender finger cupped along the side of my face as my head turned away slowly. I heard your footsteps as the violin stopped its beautiful song. A gentle sigh slid out from my lips knowing I had no chance anymore. I slowly uncovered my face and you stood directly in front of me.

"AHHHH" My voice echoed through the park before noticing it was just you, the beautiful boy that had been playing the song that was just as beautiful as you. I then heard your soft voice leave your gentle lips. "June? June Antwanette? The piano prodigy?"

I didn't even answer you but I guess you could tell from my 'oh crap' look that you were right. I wasn't sure if you knew the whole story so I'll say it now although I'm not sure if it will reach you.

I, June Antwanette was in love with piano. It all started when I heard the sounds of my own mother playing. It was a sweet tune and I suppose even my own young self knew that it would be my life. ' Tap tap tap' my footsteps rang out on the wooden floor. I stared at the piano for a long while, a gigantic wooden piano that had been the first thing my youthful eyes had ever seen. I settled myself into the leather seat. My chubby finger ran across the cold keys before playing a song my mom had been playing every day since I was born. I played it perfectly and I suppose it had been engraved into my memory. I remember the shocked look on my mom's face and that's how the real me was born.

Although, it wasn't always happy. Sometimes I'd fall asleep under the piano from long hours of work and with every mess up my mom would give me a good whack with her cane, sometimes leaving a bruise or two in place of the hit. I never had time for friends so I never made any. Eventually, my mom fell ill and was bed bound in the hospital. I had just won my first competition and ran to the hospital. She had laid there taking her dosage. I showed her the certificate and I will never forget the overwhelming amount of joy I felt when I saw her gentle smile on her face. Her words, the words that forever cursed me were "I may have to take a lot of pills but winning is the best medicine for me."

It may seem sweet when you hear it, but I was never able to live a normal life after those words. The next day in school I announced that I would be winning my next competition to make sure my mom would never have to go to the hospital again. Soon the day came, I got third place, first place for losers as my mom would say. She had come from the hospital to watch me but I could tell I hadn't made her happy. At the end of the competition, me and her met in the concrete hall. She yelled and screamed and I remember I had had enough. I screamed back the words I now wish I had never said before. "I DON'T CARE, I DON'T CARE ANYMORE I JUST WISH YOU WERE DEAD."

She died the next day. Unfortunately, for me, there was a

competition next week. When the time came, I walked onto the stage. I heard everyone whisper as I sat down that something was wrong with me because I didn't seem phased that my mom had just died. When I began to play it sounded beautiful, but then I heard my mom's voice. "You didn't play well enough for me to be here. I bet you wish you had never spoken to your mom like that." Just like that, I remember feeling like I was drowning like no light could possibly reach me. I pounded the notes as hard as I could but the crushing weight of the feeling that I was at the bottom of the ocean made the notes I played go mute. I no longer had color in my life.

Till you came into it. The moment I heard you say my name my heart sank but something inside me was relieved. I felt the pain in my chest leave me and ever since that day it has never come back. You stood there an awkward boy, thin yet with twinkling eyes and a bright youthful smile. You begged and begged for me to play a song with you at your next competition. You spoke to me as if you knew me for years yet we had just met. Did you always speak to people like that?

My heart gave a flutter and I finally just gave in letting my heart take lead as my head gave a gentle-hearted nod. I had caved in. Gosh, what was wrong with me? For months now, I've regretted this choice because maybe, just maybe, if I wouldn't have agreed then I wouldn't have lost you but now that I think about it, that wonderful feeling as a light pink tint came to your chubby cheeks. You lit up with a smile. I loved seeing you like that, that cute boy with an idiotic smile as I just gave a simple gesture. It was clear I had made your day and I felt…great about it. That feeling soon left.

The night at the competition I slowly settled myself into my seat. My breathing hitched in my throat as I struggled to stay calm. Every part of my body wanted to leap out of the auditorium but I couldn't. I had to do this for you. My hands rested on the piano. Thoughts began to race through my head as my curly red hair fell in front of my face. I stared down at the piano. You hit me with the bow of your violin. Which by the way hurt, I'll never forgive you for that.

I began to play. I remember I was nervous and I started to get that same feeling, the feeling of not being able to hear the notes and feeling the darkness surrounding me as if I were suffocating and drowning in a deep dark ocean, surrounded by flesh-eating sharks.

Suddenly, I remember hearing your song, the beautiful melody you played on your violin. I could feel the passion flowing from inside you. It filled the room with a sudden grace and it was as if you were controlling me. Suddenly through the darkness of the water, I saw the beams of light and began to swim toward them. I get it now, you were guiding me.

I remember feeling as if I were your puppet because my hands suddenly began to glide across the keys of the piano and played a song that I hadn't played in years. My fingers felt light like feathers. I closed my eyes and even then I could still play. We played as if we had practiced for years when in reality we had only practiced for about four weeks. We sat in front of an open window one night and I can't forget the words you spoke. "The world is filled with silence but it's our job to fill it with something beautiful" Those graceful words were flowing through my mind as I played but suddenly….. you dropped to the ground.

I remembered the sound as you hit the floor. It scared me to death as I quickly sprung up. You hadn't told me you were sick. I should have known, of course, you were so thin and pale. An ambulance was called. I remember the blaring sound that made my head ring. I stayed in the hospital with you for days, you only grew worse. I'd sit and read you books, draw you pictures, and sing you songs.

I could tell you were trying so hard for me. Your voice was raspy and you were always tired. I finally gave in saying the word you were probably begging for, "It's okay. I'll be fine on my own. You helped me so much but being here you will only be in pain. I love you." Like a sudden weight had been lifted, your cold hands embraced mine placing a gentle kiss on my palm.

Until you suddenly went limp…

Spring will be here soon. Spring, the season I met you, is coming.

      A spring without you...

...is coming.

Spring, without the one I fell in love with, is coming. I just hope this will reach you so you can see I'm sitting on this stage right now, for you. I can see you. I can hear you playing with me. Please don't leave again. Take me with you this time. I'm begging to hear your song one more time.

Love,
June Antwanette

# Acknowledgements

Thank you to Mr. Finlay for believing in this work. This would not have been possible without his support and leadership. It is incredible to work at a school where we have the freedom and space to take risks and to try new things.

Thank you to Mrs. Robertson for collaborating with us on this book. All of the beautiful artwork within these pages is thanks to her leadership, her flexibility with constant changes in the production process, her endless enthusiasm, and her love for the students at this school.

Thank you to Ms. Merck for helping us navigate all of the logistics involved in getting this project off the ground. Her wisdom and insight were crucial in ensuring that this endeavor did not falter in its early stages of production.

Thank you to Mr. Campbell for his unwavering support of creative writing at our school, and for inspiring many of our contributors to submit their work to this project.

Thank you to Mr. Mayes for his leadership and encouragement. He is always in our corner, encouraging us to push the limits of what is possible.

Thank you to the community that surrounds this school. Many do not realize, but this school is a very special place. None of what we do would be possible without you: the leaders, the community members, the family members, all who makeup our family here at Hughes. Thank you for your love and support and for making art like this possible.

Lastly, thank you to our students. This work is by you. It is for you. You are the reason we show up every day. You are the reason we love this job so deeply. We are so excited to see what lays ahead for you.

**The Editors**
Patrick Burell &
Toni Heyward
*March 2023*

Thank you to my wonderful wife, Ellie Burell, for your patience with me all of the days I was stressed that this project would fail or not turn out how I hoped and dreamed. Thank you for your help editing and seeing all of my blindspots when it comes to grammar and syntax.

Thank you to Mrs. Heyward for your commitment and all your work on this project. It is always a joy to collaborate with you. You believed in this on the many days that I was confident it would fall apart. No funerals.

- Patrick Burell

Thank you to Mr. Burell for trusting me to partner with you on this project. Your leadership with this project has been nothing short of phenomenal. Thank you for trusting me on this journey.

Thank you to my son, Jonah Heyward, for being an enthusiastic listener as I constantly talked about my excitement for this project.

- Toni Heyward

Made in the USA
Columbia, SC
12 April 2023